CATTLE TRAILS and COWBOYS

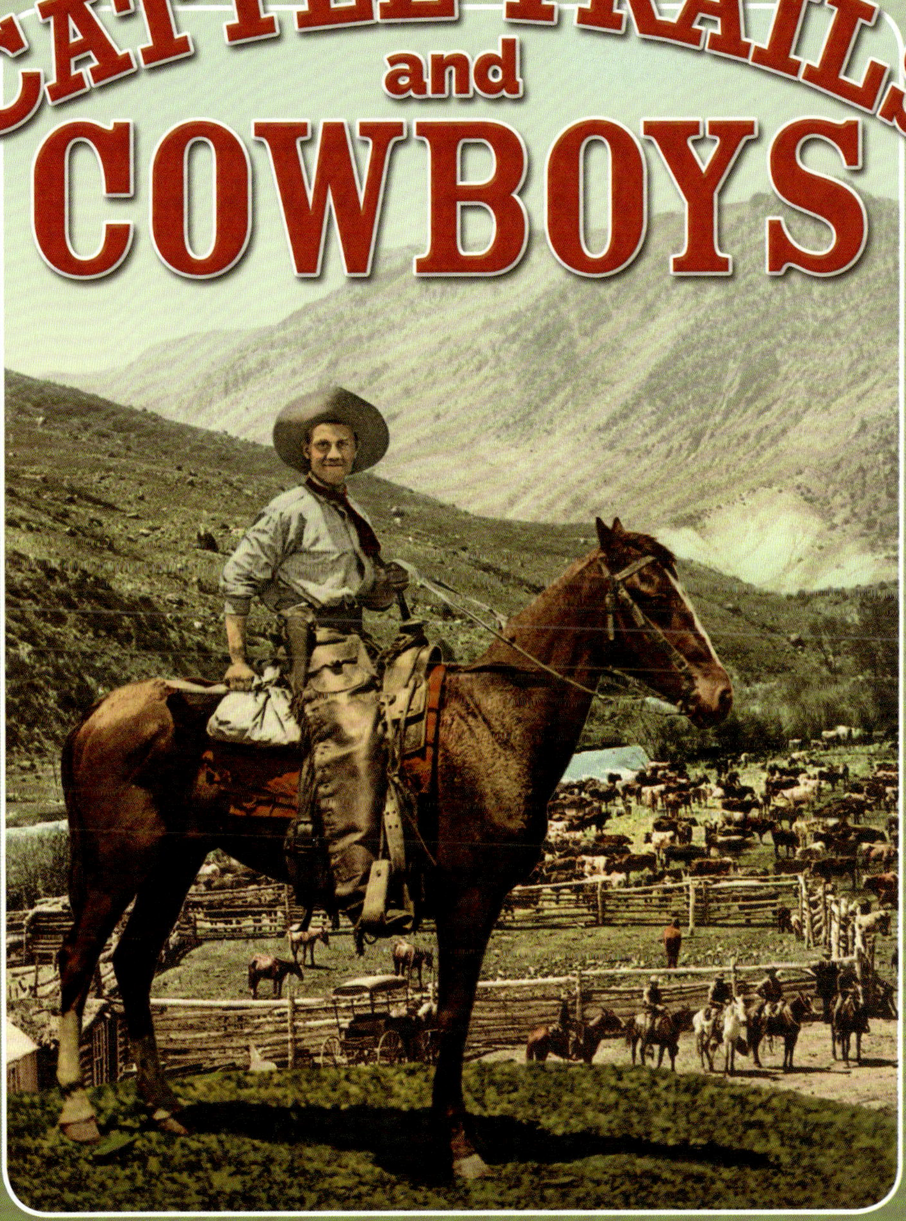

Heather E. Schwartz

Consultant

Jennifer M. Lopez, NBCT, M.S.Ed.
Teacher Specialist—History/Social Studies
Office of Curriculum & Instruction
Norfolk Public Schools

Publishing Credits

Rachelle Cracchiolo, M.S.Ed., *Publisher*
Conni Medina, M.A.Ed., *Editor in Chief*
Emily R. Smith, M.A.Ed., *Content Director*
Véronique Bos, *Creative Director*
Robin Erickson, *Art Director*
Michelle Jovin, M.A., *Associate Editor*
Kevin Panter, *Senior Graphic Designer*

Image Credits: front cover, p.1 Library of Congress [LC-DIG-ppmsca-17855]; p.4, p.5, p.14, p.16, p.17, p.32 North Wind Picture Archives; p.6 Granger Academic; p.7 (bottom) LOC [LC-USF33-003139-M3]; p.7 (top) Digital Press Photos/ Newscom; p.9 (top) LOC [LC-DIG-ppmsca-19520]; p.9 (bottom), p.11 (top), p.15 (right) U.S. National Archives; p.10 (top) LOC [LC-DIG-pga-03472]; p.10 (bottom) LOC [LC-DIG-pga-0184]; p.11 (bottom) LOC [LC-DIG-stereo-1s02762]; p.12 Chronicle/Alamy; p.13, p.28 North Wind Picture Archives/ Alamy; p.15 (left) LOC [LC-DIG-ppmsca-11406]; p.18 (top) Kansas Historical Society; p.18 (bottom), p.26 (top), p.27 Peter Newark American Pictures/Bridgeman Images; p.19 Fort Worth Star-Telegram/MCT via Getty Images; p.21 Courtesy Texas Memorial Museum; p.22 Bettmann/Getty Images; p.23 DeGolyer Library, Southern Methodist University; p.24 (top) Texas Tech University; p.24 (bottom) Documenting the American South, The University Library of the University of North Carolina at Chapel Hill; p.25 Texas State Historical Association; p.29 (top) LOC [LC-DIG-ppmsca-13514]; all other images from iStock and/or Shutterstock.

TCM Teacher Created Materials
5301 Oceanus Drive
Huntington Beach, CA 92649-1030
www.tcmpub.com

ISBN 978-0-7439-1023-1

Printed by: 590835
Printed in: China

Table of Contents

A New State

Cowboys are a long-running part of popular culture. Cattle drives appear frequently in Western movies and books. These themes are not a recent development. Instead, the story of these cowboys and their cattle drives takes place over hundreds of years. It all began in Texas.

In 1836, Texas gained its independence from Mexico. The land became a free republic for the next nine years. In 1845, Texas was annexed, or added to, the United States. It became the 28th state in the Union.

Texas was added as a slave state. The Texas Constitution of 1845 protected slavery. Like other Southern states, Texas grew dependent on cotton. It would take a nationwide war to rid the South of slavery.

enslaved people picking cotton

cotton wagons in Dallas, Texas

After the Civil War, Texas's identity evolved. Texas ranchers and cowboys helped shape the path forward. From the **antebellum** period to today, the cattle industry has played an important role in how the South—and the country as a whole—has developed.

Compromise of 1850

The Compromise of 1850 briefly settled the conflict between the North and the South. Texas gave up some western land claims in exchange for $10 million. To keep the balance between slave states and free states, California came into the Union as a free state. To satisfy the South, Congress passed a stronger version of the Fugitive Slave Act.

Fugitive Slave Act

The Fugitive Slave Act required that all runaway and escaped slaves living in Northern states be returned to their owners in the South. Antislavery people strongly opposed this law. They felt it forced them to play a part in the slave system.

1840 engraving of vaqueros lassoing cattle

Early Cattle Ranching

Cattle ranching has a long history in the United States. It began in the late 1600s. The Spanish brought longhorn cattle to Texas to feed Spanish soldiers and **missionaries**. Longhorn cattle were large and strong. Adults often weighed about 1,200 pounds (544 kilograms). The horns on their heads could span up to seven feet (over two meters)!

Mexicans living in the Texas territory were skilled in the ways of handling cattle. These Mexican ranchers were called *vaqueros* (vah-KAIR-ohs), and they used special tools to catch cattle. One tool was called a *lariat* (LAR-ee-uht), or *lasso*. This was a long rope with a noose. Vaqueros would keep the lariat near their **saddle horns**. Vaqueros were skilled, brave workers.

Early American cowboys acted and looked like Mexican vaqueros. When people from other parts of the United States moved into Texas, vaqueros taught them how to handle cattle. Vaqueros also passed on their values. Texas ranchers in the 1840s and '50s mainly ran small businesses that supplied beef to local buyers. Ranching was a small part of the Texas economy for many years. But soon, the ranching industry would experience a **boom**. It came in the form of a war.

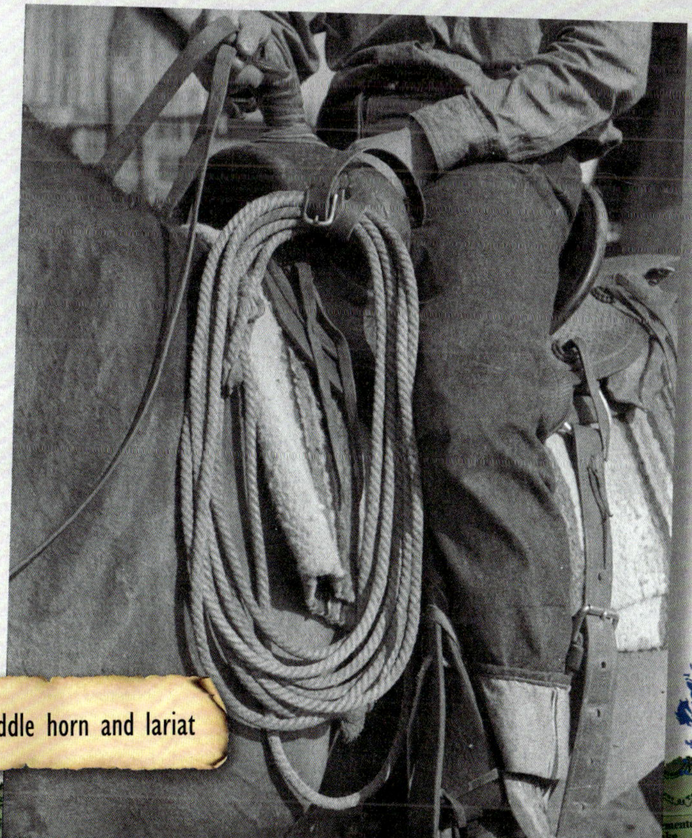

saddle horn and lariat

John Wayne became famous as a cowboy actor.

Cowboy Myths

In books and movies, cowboys are often shown as Southern white men. In actuality, most Texas cowboys were mestizo. *Mestizo* refers to a person of mixed racial ancestry, particularly of Spanish and **indigenous** ancestry.

Lariat

The word *lariat* comes from the Spanish words *la reata*. That simply means "the rope." When Spanish-speaking cowboys said to get "la reata," they really just meant get any rope.

The Civil War

The issue of slavery had been at the heart of American politics for decades. With each new state came the same question: will it be a slave state or a free state? The **rift** between the North and the South was growing with each passing year.

In November 1860, Abraham Lincoln was elected president. He was against slavery expanding west. Several slave states **seceded** and formed the Confederate States of America. They claimed that all Union forts in the South now belonged to the Confederacy. In March 1861, Confederate troops surrounded Fort Sumter in South Carolina. They demanded Union troops leave. The fort's leader

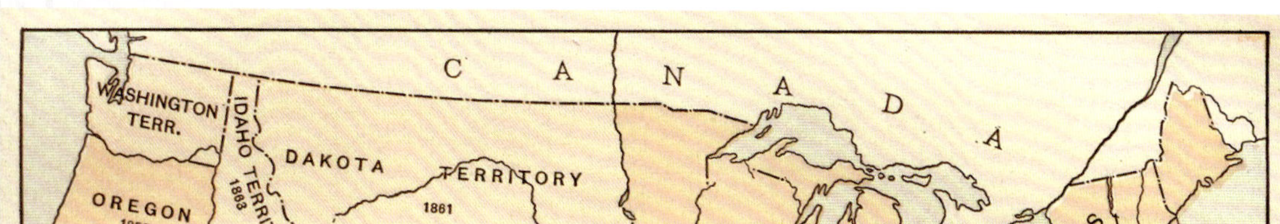

the United States during the Civil War

the attack on Fort Sumter, 1861

refused, so the Confederates opened fire. After less than two days of fighting, Union forces surrendered. The Confederates felt they had been forced into attacking since the Union troops would not leave. The Union felt that Confederates started the war by attacking a **federal** fort. The Battle of Fort Sumter was the tipping point between the North and the South. By the summer of 1861, all of the South had seceded. The Civil War had begun.

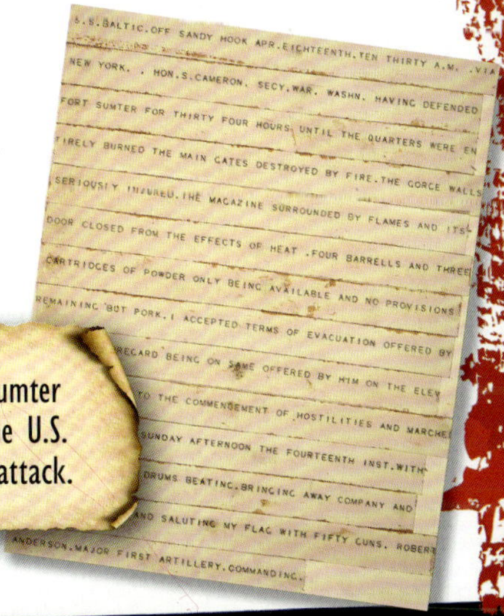

S.S.BALTIC.OFF SANDY HOOK APR.EIGHTEENTH.TEN THIRTY A.M. .VIA
NEW YORK. . HON.S.CAMERON. SECY.WAR. WASHN. HAVING DEFENDED
FORT SUMTER FOR THIRTY FOUR HOURS UNTIL THE QUARTERS WERE EN
TIRELY BURNED THE MAIN GATES DESTROYED BY FIRE.THE GORGE WALLS
SERIOUSLY INJURED.THE MAGAZINE SURROUNDED BY FLAMES AND ITS
DOOR CLOSED FROM THE EFFECTS OF HEAT .FOUR BARRELLS AND THREE
CARTRIDGES OF POWDER ONLY BEING AVAILABLE AND NO PROVISIONS
REMAINING BUT PORK.I ACCEPTED TERMS OF EVACUATION OFFERED BY
REGARD BEING ON SAME OFFERED BY HIM ON THE ELEV
TO THE COMMENCEMENT OF HOSTILITIES AND MARCHE
SUNDAY AFTERNOON THE FOURTEENTH INST.WITH
DRUMS BEATING.BRINGING AWAY COMPANY AND
AND SALUTING MY FLAG WITH FIFTY GUNS. ROBERT
ANDERSON.MAJOR FIRST ARTILLERY.COMMANDING.

The Union leader at Fort Sumter sent this telegram to tell the U.S. secretary of war about the attack.

The Election of 1860

Lincoln's victory in the 1860 presidential election came almost entirely from the North, the Midwest, and the West. He was not elected by a single slave state. It would have been hard to do, considering 10 out of the 15 slave states didn't even put his name on the ballot!

The Lone Death

On April 14, Union troops left Fort Sumter waving the American flag. Confederate troops began a 100-gun salute to celebrate their victory. A cannon accidentally went off early, causing an explosion. Union Private Daniel Hough was killed. While he did not die during battle, Hough is still considered the first **casualty** of the Civil War.

The North thought it would defeat the South quickly. Southern General Robert E. Lee made sure that did not happen. For the first year, Lee defended Virginia. In other places, though, the Union was winning key battles. Both sides remained in a **stalemate**. Southern troops were losing soldiers to injury and **desertion**. By 1862, the course of the war was beginning to change.

In July, Lincoln drafted an announcement. It stated that the seceded states had to come back to the Union. If they didn't, all enslaved people in those states would be freed. Lincoln finished his draft but did not immediately issue it. He did not want his announcement to be seen as a sign that the North was losing and was desperate for the war to end. So, he put the document away in his desk.

Lincoln

Then, in September, the Battle of Antietam took place. Both sides had heavy losses, but Lincoln saw it as a Union victory. So, he issued his document—the Emancipation Proclamation.

the Battle of Antietam

Despite the proclamation, no Southern states rejoined the Union. The order went into effect on January 1, 1863. The Confederates did not honor the law, so no enslaved people in the South were freed. However, the proclamation also let African Americans join the Union military for the first time.

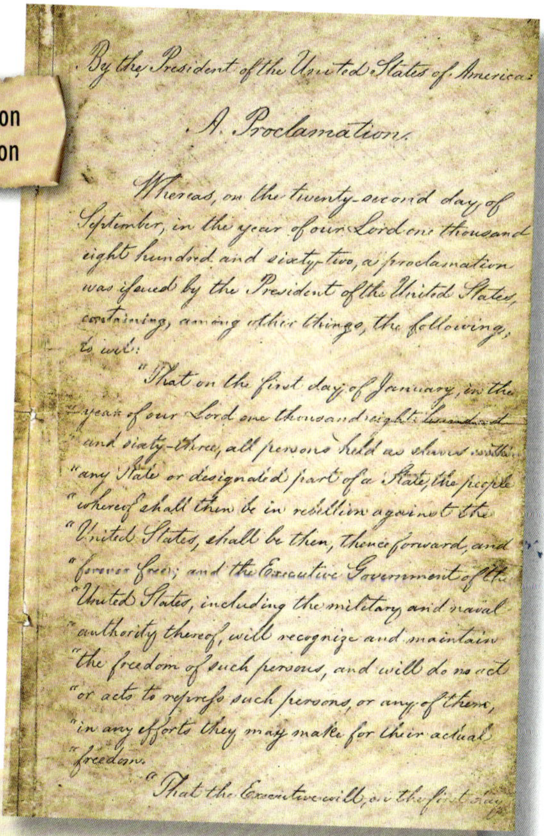
By the President of the United States of America:

A Proclamation.

Whereas, on the twenty-second day of September, in the year of our Lord one thousand eight hundred and sixty-two, a proclamation was issued by the President of the United States, containing, among other things, the following, to wit:

"That on the first day of January, in the year of our Lord one thousand eight hundred and sixty-three, all persons held as slaves within "any State or designated part of a State, the people "whereof shall then be in rebellion against the "United States, shall be then, thenceforward, and "forever free; and the Executive Government of the "United States, including the military and naval "authority thereof, will recognize and maintain "the freedom of such persons, and will do no act "or acts to repress such persons, or any of them, "in any efforts they may make for their actual "freedom.

"That the Executive will, on the first day

Emancipation Proclamation

These Union soldiers used to be enslaved.

Antietam

About 132,000 soldiers faced off in the early hours of September 17, 1862, at the Battle of Antietam. There were nearly 23,000 casualties in one day. The following day, both sides were too bloodied to fight. On the night of September 18 and into the 19, Lee and his men **retreated**. Officially, the bloodiest day in American military history ended in a tie. But since Lee retreated, Lincoln saw it as a win for the Union.

In the Military

More than 200,000 African Americans joined the Union army and navy. These brave men also had to deal with an additional risk that white soldiers did not—if they were captured while in the South, they could be forced into slavery.

Freedom at Last

On July 1, 1863, Confederate and Union forces met in the Battle of Gettysburg. Gettysburg was fought over the course of three days. In the end, one-fourth of the Union soldiers and one-half of the Confederate soldiers were severely injured or killed.

By 1865, the Union was firmly winning the war. Union troops had stretched Lee's **dwindling** forces thin. On March 25, Lee tried to attack Union troops at Ford Stedman in Virginia. The plan failed, and Lee was forced to retreat while the Union army chased after him. The chase lasted for 88 miles (142 kilometers) until the injured Confederate forces ran out of food. Lee surrendered his troops on April 9 in Appomattox Court House, Virginia.

the Battle of Gettysburg

While Lee only surrendered his forces, the entire Confederate army soon followed. The last Confederate **ports** were handed over on June 2. The Civil War was over.

Historians do not have exact numbers in regard to the Civil War. However, it is widely believed that around 1,556,000 soldiers served the Union. About one in four died. Around 800,000 soldiers served the Confederacy. About one in three of those soldiers died. By the end of the war, two percent of all Americans had died as a direct result of the war.

Lincoln's Speech

On November 19, 1863, President Lincoln attended a funeral at the Gettysburg battleground. He gave a 272-word speech called the Gettysburg Address. In it, Lincoln wondered if the United States could continue as a united nation. He asked that both sides remember the Founding Fathers' ideas of liberty and equality. The speech was widely praised and quickly became famous around the world.

Lee's Surrender

General Lee's surrender to Union General Ulysses S. Grant only took about 90 minutes. Grant told his men to stop firing celebratory cannon shots. Grant also offered to feed Lee's troops and did not arrest anyone. The bloodiest war in American history ended in a peaceful way.

Rebuilding the South

The death and destruction of the Civil War had widespread and long-lasting effects on the country. After the Civil War, the United States went through many changes. This period of change after the war was called Reconstruction.

In the spring of 1865, the U.S. Army took control of the eleven Southern states. The goal was to protect **emancipated**, or freed, African Americans. Freedom meant new kinds of relations between black and white people in the South. Many white people did not treat formerly enslaved people as their equals. The U.S. government wanted to make sure the South would be loyal to the nation and would respect their new ways of living.

Black men vote in the South for the first time.

Some of these buffalo soldiers wear coats made of buffalo fur.

In 1866, four **regiments** of African American troops were added to the U.S. Army. These soldiers helped rebuild and enforce the new rules. American Indians called these troops "buffalo soldiers." Historians aren't sure why that name was chosen. It could have been because some of the soldiers wore coats made of buffalo fur. Or, it could have been because the soldiers fought fiercely, like buffalo did. In any case, buffalo soldiers helped the new nation grow as one.

Flipper

Trailblazer

Henry O. Flipper was born into slavery in 1856. In 1877, he became the first African American to graduate from the United States Military Academy at West Point. He also became the first African American officer to lead the buffalo soldiers.

New Farmers

During Reconstruction, a system known as *sharecropping* emerged. Under this system, poor farmers could rent land from wealthy landowners. Payment came from the crops they harvested. Sadly, landowners often charged high rates to rent tools, thereby forcing the farmers into **debt**.

The Rise of the Cattle Industry

cowboys on a cattle drive from Texas to Kansas in the 1870s

The Texas cattle industry began to grow during Reconstruction. There had been cattle drives before the Civil War, but the war had blocked access to northern and eastern cities. After the war, Texas ranchers saw an opportunity to open the trails again. In Texas, each **head** of cattle was worth about $5–10. (That was if ranchers could even find someone to buy it.) However, people in northern cities, such as Chicago and Cincinnati, would pay $40 for that same head of cattle. Cattle were worth even more in the West. Gold miners in San Francisco would pay up to $200 per head!

So, in 1866, ranchers started hiring cowboys to drive their cattle to states where livestock was sold at higher prices. Ranchers were eager to send their cattle out of Texas and make more money. Soon, hundreds of thousands of cattle were on trails heading out of Texas.

cowboys eating from a chuck wagon

Cooks and Cowboys

The leaders of cattle drives, called "trail bosses," made the most money. They were paid around $100 each month they were on the trails. The next highest-paid person on a crew was the cook, who earned about $60 per month.

Charles's Kitchen

In 1866, rancher Charles Goodnight created a portable kitchen to take on long cattle drives. The "chuck wagon" carried bed rolls, lanterns, food, coffee, water, cooking utensils, and other necessities. The cook was in charge of the chuck wagon. Before the cook went to sleep each night, he had to turn the chuck wagon toward the North Star so the trail boss could determine directions in the morning.

The Chisholm Trail

As cattle drives became more and more popular, cowboys **blazed** new trails. One of those trails became known as the Chisholm Trail.

Chisholm

In 1865, two men named Jesse Chisholm and James R. Mead built a trading post in present-day Oklahoma City. As cattle drives began to happen more frequently, their trading post became popular. Soon, the trading post became a connection point between Texas ranches and markets in Kansas. A path soon formed. It began south of San Antonio, Texas, and ran north through Oklahoma. The trail ended in Abilene, Kansas. In 1867, a new cattle-shipping **depot** opened along the railroad in Kansas. Suddenly, the Chisholm Trail (as it came to be known) was overflowing with cowboys and cattle. Between 1867 and 1871, about 1.5 million head of cattle were driven along the Chisholm Trail.

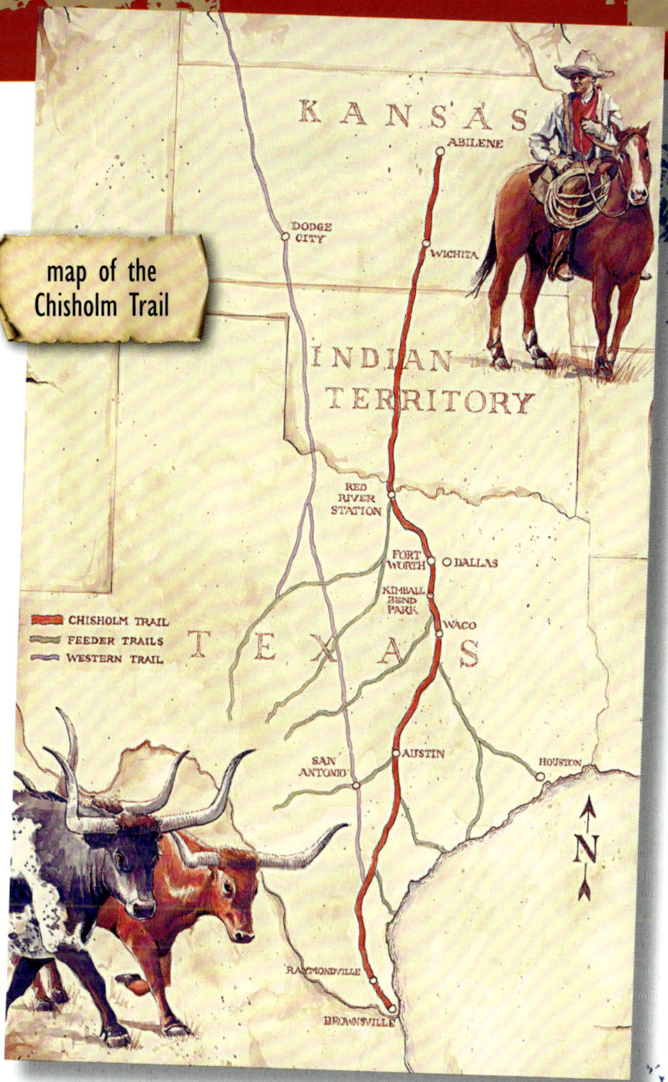

map of the Chisholm Trail

Over the next few years, the Chisholm Trail declined in popularity. Other routes were formed and new railroad depots were opened, so the trail wasn't as important as it once was. However, in the 1880s, the Santa Fe Railroad reached Kentucky. Cowboys used the Chisholm Trail to reach the railroad and send cattle north. The trail remained popular until the decline of long-distance cattle drives.

Chisholm's Skills

Jesse Chisholm worked as a trader for half his life. His interactions with many different people taught him to speak and understand more than 10 languages. Chisholm became a popular guide and translator. During the Civil War, he worked with local American Indian tribes on behalf of the Confederacy and as a translator on behalf of the Union.

Texas Fever

Kansas farmers complained that cattle from Texas were getting their cattle sick. The so-called "Texas fever" caused the government to take action. Ranchers could still bring their Texas cattle to Kansas from December through February (when the disease was not as widespread), but they were **banned** for the rest of the year. Texas fever was one of the reasons the Chisholm Trail lost its popularity.

The Great Western Cattle Trail

Just as the Chisholm Trail was declining in popularity, another trail was on the rise. In 1874, cattle driver John T. Lytle drove 3,500 head of cattle from southern Texas to Fort Robinson, Nebraska. Other cowboys soon followed his path. With that, the Great Western Cattle Trail was born, stretching from southern Texas to Nebraska.

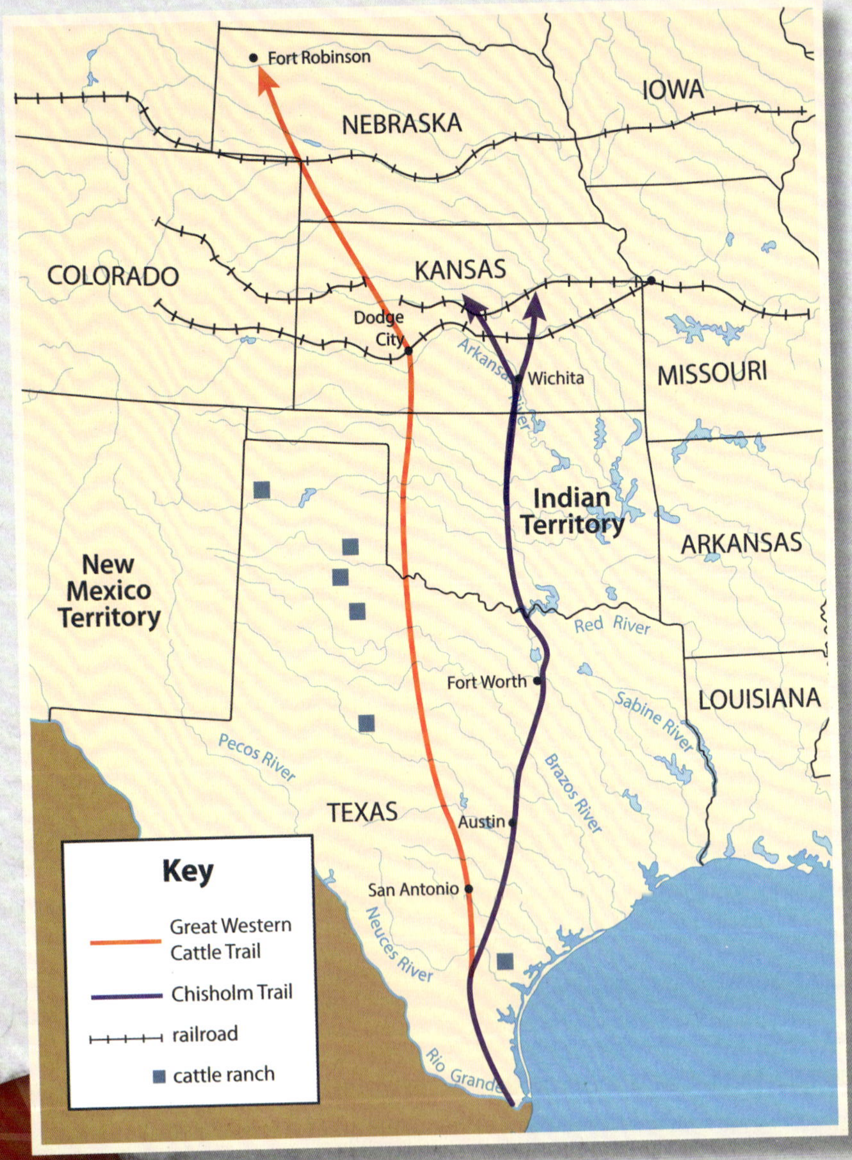

The Great Western Cattle Trail ran parallel to the Chisholm Trail. However, the Great Western Cattle Trail was farther west. This proved to be a very important difference.

From 1874 to 1875, the U.S. Army removed American Indians from the southern Plains and forced them to move to **reservations**. American ranchers quickly moved to the now-empty Texas **panhandle**. The Great Western Cattle Trail was closer and proved to be more convenient than the Chisholm Trail.

The Great Western Cattle Trail was in use until 1893. By then, between three and five million head of cattle had been driven along its route.

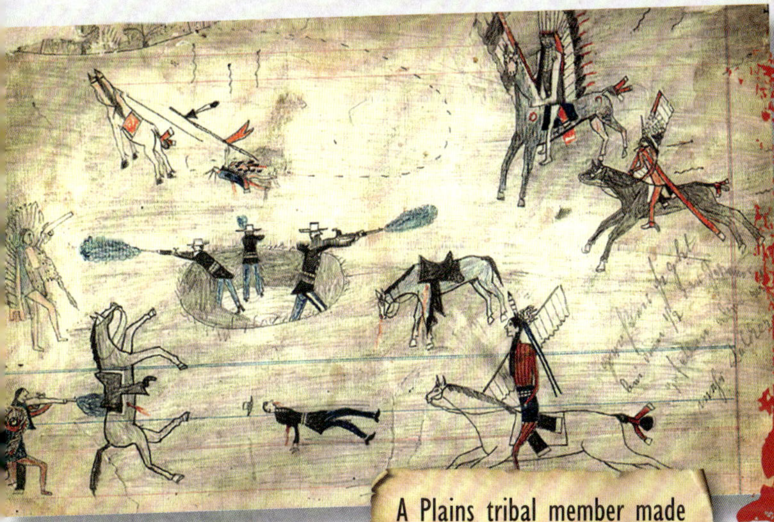

A Plains tribal member made this drawing of a battle in the Red River War.

Red River War

In 1867, several American Indian tribes in the Plains signed a **treaty** with the U.S. government. These tribes agreed to move to reservations, while the government agreed to give food to the tribes and to keep settlers off their lands. However, the government rarely enforced the treaty. Settlers went onto reservations and killed most of the bison living there. The tribes relied on bison for food and supplies, so the tribes attempted to leave the reservations. They also joined other tribes in attacking bison hunters. The U.S. Army was sent in to stop the tribes. After a year of fighting, the last of the tribes surrendered on June 2, 1875, and were forced to live on reservations. The Red River War proved to be the end of free-roaming Plains tribes.

Cowboy Life

Cattle drives often covered 10–15 mi. (16–24 km) each day and could take anywhere from 25 to 100 days to complete. Cattle were not easy to control on drives. They spread out into long lines that could be hard to manage. Some lines could be up to 6 mi. (10 km) long! To keep cattle in line, cowboys surrounded the animals at different points. They communicated with their fellow workers by using hand signals borrowed from American Indian sign language. They also gestured with their hats.

Cowboys worked in crews of about 12 people and managed 2,000–3,000 head of cattle per drive. A 12-person crew usually had a trail boss, a cook, and about 10 wranglers and drovers. Wranglers were in charge of keeping the spare horses healthy and fed. This was a tough job since most wranglers were in charge of more than one hundred horses at a time! Drovers kept the cattle in line. All these cowboys had to be very skilled riders.

Lizzie Johnson

Take Your Positions

Trail bosses assigned drovers to different positions around the herd. The *point* rode in front of the herd and kept them going in the right direction. The *swings* rode alongside the widest parts of the herd and chased after any cattle that walked out of line. The *flanks* rode farther back and helped the swings when they had to chase stray cattle. Lastly, the *drag* rode behind the herd and kept the cattle moving forward. The drag was the least desirable position since they got a face full of dust the entire way!

Cowgirls on the Trails

One of the most successful cowgirls of the late 19th century was Lizzie Johnson. She bought her own herd and had her own **brand**. She is believed to be the first woman to drive her herd along the Chisholm Trail.

Wallace

Rancher Wallace

Daniel Webster Wallace was born to enslaved parents. When he was 17, he ran away and joined a cattle drive. Wallace worked for years until he saved up enough money to buy his own ranch. His skills earned him the respect of his fellow ranchers. When Wallace died in 1939, he left behind property that was worth more than $1 million (about $18 million in today's money).

A New Generation

When Cleo Hearn was young, he was not allowed to compete in rodeos until after the crowd had left. Hearn wanted to honor the black cowboys of Texas and give all children an equal opportunity. So, he began the Cowboys of Color Rodeo. Today, the touring rodeo features more than 200 cowboys and cowgirls who compete at rodeos in the South.

The Black Cowboys of Texas

Cowboys came from different walks of life. Civil War veterans became cowboys. Formerly enslaved people became cowboys. Runaways became cowboys too. No matter where they came from, cowboys had to be strong and tough to handle their jobs.

Nat Love was born into slavery and became a famous black cowboy.

In the late 1800s, one-fourth of working cowboys in Texas were black. Many of these cowboys had been born into slavery. When enslavers went to fight in the Civil War, they left their enslaved people behind to take care of the cattle and horses. These enslaved people learned how to manage the land and huge herds of cattle.

After the Civil War, many "black cowboys" found work on ranches where they were formerly enslaved. When the long cattle drives began, black cowboys' skills were in high demand. Along the trails, black cowboys were often treated poorly in the towns they passed through. However, among the crew, black cowboys were typically treated with the level of respect owed to them.

Cattle drives were dangerous and all cowboys had to overcome risks. However, black cowboys had many obstacles that their white counterparts did not have to face. That is what makes their success stories truly remarkable.

Cowboys try to outrun a cattle stampede.

Dangers on the Trail

All cowboys faced harsh conditions on cattle drives. They had to handle their herds in all kinds of weather. During dry times, they struggled to find water for the animals and for themselves. During rainy periods, they had trouble crossing flooded rivers. Drowning was a real threat. Lightning and thunder could also cause problems by scaring cattle. Frightened cattle sometimes led to a **stampede**. The animals would run wild and scatter. Before they were rounded up, they could easily kill cowboys by trampling them.

There were other dangers on the trails too. Along the trails, thieves could attack the herds and try to steal the cattle for themselves. Cowboys also had to watch out for rattlesnakes. A rattlesnake bite could be deadly if not treated properly.

rattlesnake

When cowboys were injured or became ill on trails, they had to rely on homemade cures. A typical cure for a rattlesnake bite in the 1800s was to cut the skin around the bite. Then, the poison could be squeezed or sucked out of the wound. When cowboys got other kinds of wounds, they applied a prickly pear cactus **poultice**. To stay healthy on the trail, cowboys often drank bison-meat juice!

a railroad construction crew in 1886

Stampede!

To stop a stampede, the cowboy closest to the front of the herd would ride in front of the cattle and force the cattle to turn right. Other cowboys would keep forcing the cattle to turn right until the cattle were running in a circle. Then, cowboys would start closing in on the circle until the cattle were forced to slow to a walk.

Expanding Railroads

Railroad construction after the Civil War extended train service into new territories. Railroad expansion changed the West. New towns sprang up and old towns died off as railroads stretched across the country.

End of an Era

Cattle drives did not last as a major part of the western economy. Problems with the system began with Texas fever in the 1850s. Some Texan cattle carried a deadly disease that could spread to other cattle. So, cattle from Texas were banned from entering some states. Harsh winters in the late 1880s made travel by trail very dangerous. New railroads meant there was less need to drive cattle to distant markets. The meat could now be shipped to other states in refrigerated train cars.

Cowboys herd Texas longhorn into a train car.

poster for Buffalo Bill's Wild West show

By the 1900s, cowboys who roamed the open range were a thing of the past. Some cowboys joined Wild West shows. In these shows, they could use their skills to perform for audiences. Over time, Wild West shows evolved into rodeo shows. In this way, the cowboy **legacy** continues to live on in the South.

modern rodeo show

The Wild West

In 1883, William F. Cody, also known as Buffalo Bill, organized Buffalo Bill's Wild West show. His show featured famous cowboys, cowgirls, and American Indians. They traveled all over the United States showcasing their incredible skills.

Barbed Wire

The widespread use of barbed wire in the 1880s also led to the end of cattle drives. Barbed wire divided up the open range. Cattle could no longer pass freely over trails where there were barbed wire fences.

barbed wire

Glossary

antebellum—occurring in the U.S. South before the Civil War

banned—ordered not to do something

blazed—created a route

boom—sudden growth in an economic industry in a short period of time

brand—a distinctive mark that is burned into the skin of an animal to show who owns the animal

casualty—a person who is killed, captured, or seriously injured during warfare

debt—a state of owing another

depot—a regular stopping point for travelers

desertion—the act of leaving the military without permission and without the intention of returning

dwindling—gradually becoming smaller

emancipated—freed from slavery or from someone else's control

federal—relating to the main government of a place

head—an individual animal

indigenous—refers to those whose ancestors were among the first people to live in a place

legacy—something that happened in the past or comes from the past

missionaries—people who are sent to foreign places to do religious work

panhandle—a narrow strip of land that extends out from a larger territory, such as a state

ports—places where ships dock and load and unload cargo

poultice—a soft, usually heated substance that is put on a piece of cloth and then placed on skin to reduce pain or heal sores

regiments—military units made of several large groups of soldiers

reservations—areas of land in the United States that are kept separate as places for American Indians to live

retreated—moved away from the threat of danger or attack

rift—a situation in which two groups or people no longer have a friendly relationship

saddle horns—leather grips found near the front of some saddles

seceded—separated from a nation and became independent

stalemate—a situation in which neither side can gain an advantage or win

stampede—an occurrence in which a large group of scared or excited animals run together in a wild and uncontrolled way

treaty—an official agreement made between two or more countries or groups

Index

Your Turn!

After the Civil War, many people found success working as cowboys. Cowboys on cattle drives worked long hours for months at a time. Jobs on the trails included keeping the cattle in line, watching for thieves, keeping horses fed and healthy, administering medicine, and cooking.

Design a poster advertising jobs for an upcoming cattle drive. Be sure to list the positives about joining a cattle drive and the different opportunities open to interested applicants.